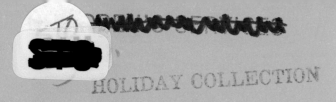

M. C. HELLDORFER

Daniel's Gift

ILLUSTRATED BY JULIE DOWNING

BRADBURY PRESS   NEW YORK

10 9 8 7 6 5 4 3 2 1

Library of Congress Cataloging-in-Publication Data   Helldorfer, Mary-Claire, 1954-   Daniel's gift.   Summary: Three shepherd boys guard their sheep in the hills near Bethlehem the night Jesus is born. 1. Jesus Christ—Nativity—Juvenile fiction. [1. Jesus Christ—Nativity—Fiction] I. Downing, Julie, ill. II. Title.   PZ7.H37418Dan 1987   [E]   87-5160   ISBN 0-02-743511-3

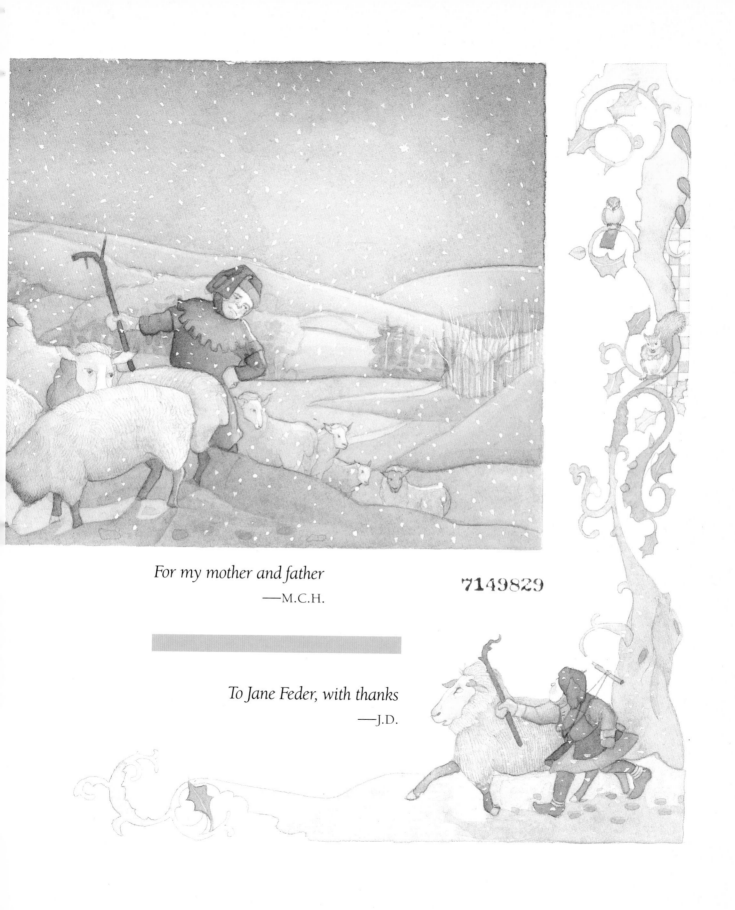

For my mother and father
—M.C.H.

To Jane Feder, with thanks
—J.D.

One winter night, when a star shone brighter than the sun
and moon, three brothers watched over their sheep. They
were cold and tired but could not go home to sleep.

The middle boy said to the oldest, "Too bad for us Daniel is such a dreamer. We
could never trust him alone with the flock."

"Daniel watches stars, not sheep," Rafe replied. "If we didn't watch him, he'd wander off."

"Following a song he hears." Zeke poked the boy. "Then what if Mak the sheep-stealer comes?"

Daniel sprang up. "I'm big! I am, and can guard the sheep all alone. I can! I can!" he said, dancing about in the field.

"Well," said Rafe, "we shall see." He winked at Zeke, and the two lazy brothers rolled over to snore.

As soon as they did, Daniel began to play his wooden pipe. His favorite sheep snuggled next to him and blinked his shiny eyes.

"Look, Mammoth," the boy said, pointing to the great star. "One new, and brighter than the rest. We may see some wonder tonight." Then Daniel made up a dreaming song that told of the birth of a shepherd king.

Suddenly he heard the trees move behind him. A man stepped out, cloaked in black, his eyes dark as caves. Over his shoulder hung an empty sack.

Daniel called loudly, "Who's there?"

"Quiet, child. Just a traveler. Don't be afraid." The man's face was full of shadows. "Let me stay a while with you. I know amazing stories of the births and deaths of all-powerful kings."

Crouching close to the boy and his sheep, the stranger
droned long about the ancient battles of mighty lords.
    Daniel scratched his sheep and nodded, and nodded again.
Then his hand slipped from Mammoth and

he fell fast asleep.

Daniel slept until

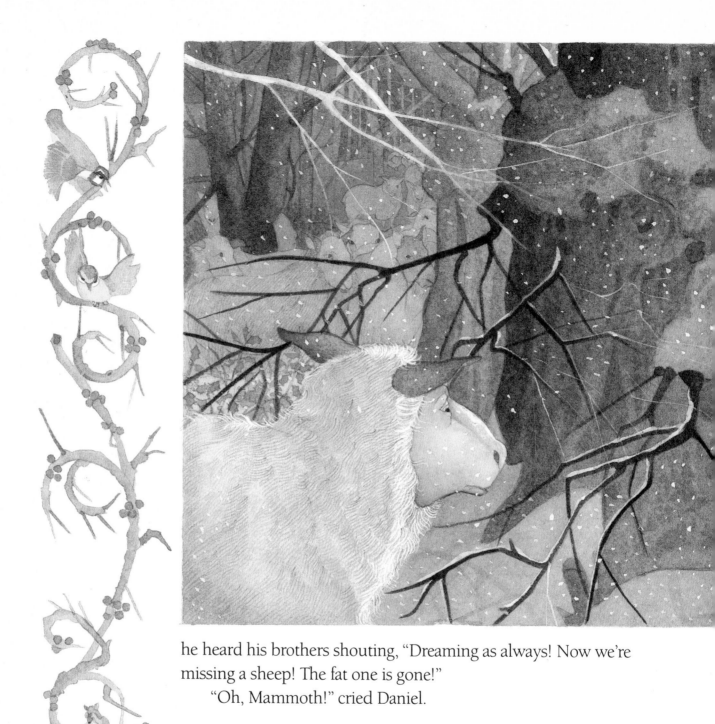

he heard his brothers shouting, "Dreaming as always! Now we're missing a sheep! The fat one is gone!"

"Oh, Mammoth!" cried Daniel.

His brothers were furious, and pounded him all the way to the house of Mak the sheep-stealer.

"If that old butcher has already cooked him…," Rafe threatened.

At Mak's cottage all the windows were shuttered. They banged on the door.

"Quiet!" called the man inside. "My wife is tired and sick, and all night I've been here singing our newborn asleep." He croaked a tune: *"Lully lullaye."*

"Where's our sheep?" asked Zeke, pushing his way through the door. The three boys searched Mak's house—the lofts, the cubbies, under tables and beds.

Mak's wife held her stomach and wailed, "*Oooo*. Let a poor woman and her new baby sleep."

Mak glared and rocked the cradle. No one could find the sheep.

"They've already eaten him," said Rafe.

A tear started down Daniel's cheek. He stumbled out the door behind his brothers.

"That baby will grow up as bad as his father," Rafe said to Zeke.

Then Daniel remembered. "We did not give Mak's baby a gift."

"You wool brain!" Zeke and Rafe exclaimed. "Mak stole our sheep and you want to give his baby a gift?"

But Daniel knew all babies should have gifts. He searched his pocket, then knocked on Mak's door.

"Go away!" hissed Mak.

"I have a gift," the boy whispered.

"THE BABY'S SLEEPING!" shouted Mak.

"…Did you say gift?" He opened the door and smiled.

Daniel held out his shepherd's pipe.

"That?" thundered Mak. "You call that a gift?" Snatching it he blew one ugly note.

From the cradle came a strange reply.

"He's awake!" the boy said. Taking back his pipe, he ducked under Mak's arms.

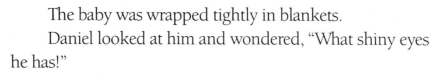

The baby was wrapped tightly in blankets.

Daniel looked at him and wondered, "What shiny eyes he has!"

"Like mine!" snapped Mak.

"And what a long, long nose," the boy said.

"My wife's," replied Mak.

"And what funny, furry toes."

"Like—"

"Mammoth's!" the boy cried. Snatching up his sheep, he ran out the door.

In their field once again, the older brothers
quarreled. "You stay up and watch with Daniel," said
Rafe. "I'm more tired than I was before."

Zeke refused. "He's slept and dreamed enough
tonight. This time he'll stay awake."

So the two lazy boys rolled over to snore and Daniel sat with Mammoth, keeping their flock.

Suddenly, he saw a flurry of light. The boy sprang up, clutching Mammoth to him.

"Who's there?" he called out.

A man whose face shone like a star!

"Do not be afraid," the stranger said. "I bring you good news. This night a child is born. He is King of kings, Shepherd of men. He lies now in a sheep's crib in Bethlehem."

The stranger vanished.

Daniel woke his brothers to tell them what he had seen and heard. They were very angry. "Do not disturb us!" they said, jabbing him in the ribs. "Dreamer, dreamer, dreamer," they shouted. "Woolly in the head!"

But Daniel didn't listen. He picked up Mammoth and ran down the hillside, following the great star's light. His brothers waved their arms and chased him, like people from a nightmare.

Far into town Daniel ran, up and down streets, his heart pounding against Mammoth. By a stable's open door he stopped.

Music stirred the air like a hundred wings. In a soft hay bed lay a baby, his father bending near. His mother leaned against a sleeping donkey. Three grandfather-shepherds kept watch.

The father looked up. "Come in," he called.

Holding tightly to Mammoth, Daniel stepped closer.

"Come see our baby," said the mother.

"But, I have nothing to give him, just the wooden pipe I play for my sheep."

The baby smiled up at the boy.

"It's a fine gift," said the father, taking the pipe.

He began to play and Daniel rested his head against
Mammoth,

        listening,

                until he fell asleep.

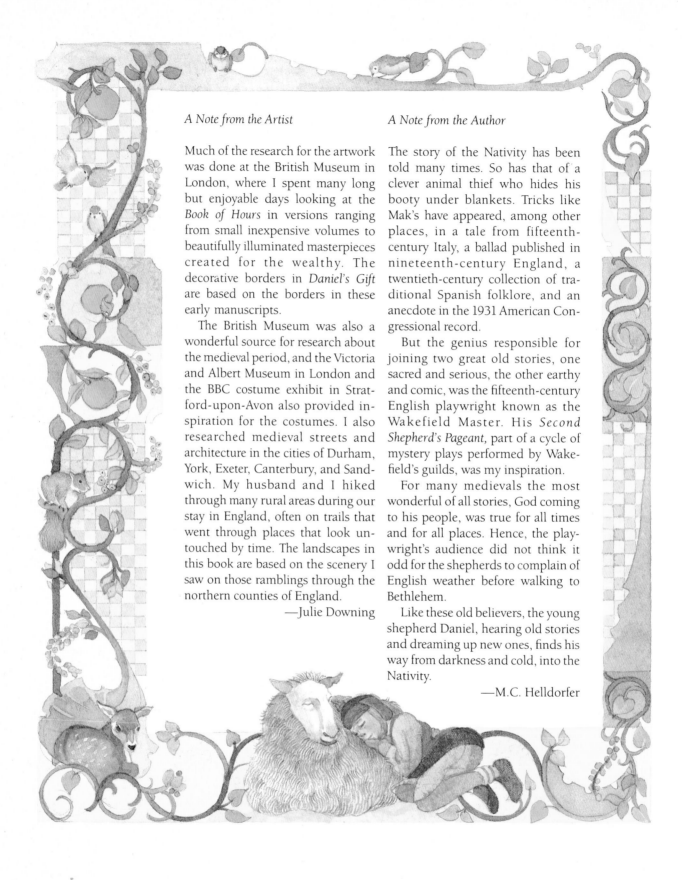

A Note from the Artist

Much of the research for the artwork was done at the British Museum in London, where I spent many long but enjoyable days looking at the *Book of Hours* in versions ranging from small inexpensive volumes to beautifully illuminated masterpieces created for the wealthy. The decorative borders in *Daniel's Gift* are based on the borders in these early manuscripts.

The British Museum was also a wonderful source for research about the medieval period, and the Victoria and Albert Museum in London and the BBC costume exhibit in Stratford-upon-Avon also provided inspiration for the costumes. I also researched medieval streets and architecture in the cities of Durham, York, Exeter, Canterbury, and Sandwich. My husband and I hiked through many rural areas during our stay in England, often on trails that went through places that look untouched by time. The landscapes in this book are based on the scenery I saw on those ramblings through the northern counties of England.

—Julie Downing

A Note from the Author

The story of the Nativity has been told many times. So has that of a clever animal thief who hides his booty under blankets. Tricks like Mak's have appeared, among other places, in a tale from fifteenth-century Italy, a ballad published in nineteenth-century England, a twentieth-century collection of traditional Spanish folklore, and an anecdote in the 1931 American Congressional record.

But the genius responsible for joining two great old stories, one sacred and serious, the other earthy and comic, was the fifteenth-century English playwright known as the Wakefield Master. His *Second Shepherd's Pageant,* part of a cycle of mystery plays performed by Wakefield's guilds, was my inspiration.

For many medievals the most wonderful of all stories, God coming to his people, was true for all times and for all places. Hence, the playwright's audience did not think it odd for the shepherds to complain of English weather before walking to Bethlehem.

Like these old believers, the young shepherd Daniel, hearing old stories and dreaming up new ones, finds his way from darkness and cold, into the Nativity.

—M.C. Helldorfer